To all the parents struggling to protect their children and elevate their souls—with love
—L.S.

To my dad, for being funny, being strong, and helping me to follow suit
—D.M.

But I Waaannt It!

Text copyright © 2000 by Dr. Laura Schlessinger

Illustrations copyright © 2000 by Daniel McFeeley

Printed in the United States. All rights reserved.

www.harperchildrens.com

Library of Congress Cataloging-in-Publication Data

Schlessinger, Laura.

But I waaannt it! / by Laura Schlessinger ; illustrated by Daniel McFeeley. — 1st ed.

p. cm.

Summary: After his mother buys him all the stuffed animals he wants, a boy discovers what he truly wants.

ISBN 0-06-028775-6. — ISBN 0-06-028958-9 (lib. bdg.)

[1. Greed—Fiction. 2. Conduct of life—Fiction.] I. McFeeley, Dan, ill. II. Title.

PZ7.S347115Bu 2000

[E]—dc21

99-37140

CIP

1 2 3 4 5 6 7 8 9 10

First Edition

Dr. Laura Schlessinger's

But I WAAANNT it!

Illustrated by Daniel McFeeley

Cliff Street Books
An Imprint of HarperCollinsPublishers

"Come on, Sammy, we're going to the toy store," said Mother. "I'd like you to help pick out a stuffed animal for your cousin Rachel. It's her second birthday."

"Wow," yelled Sammy, "I'm going to the toy store. Cool! Awesome! Let's go! Come on, Mommy, hurry!"

Mother looked at all the toys. "Oh my," she said. "Look at how many different stuffed animals there are. I wonder which one will be just right for Rachel? Sammy, why don't you decide which one to buy?"

But Sammy wasn't listening. "I want this gorilla and this giraffe and this dog and this parrot and . . ."

"I'm sorry, Sammy, but we came here only to get your cousin Rachel a present," said Mother. "We won't be buying anything for you today."

"But I *waaannt* it!" Sammy screeched, as he pulled on the toy Mother was putting back on the shelf. "I want *all* of them!"

"Honey, calm down and tell me why you want them so much," Mother said.

"Because," Sammy sniffled, "having them all will make me so *verrry* happy."

"Really?" said Mother. "Let's see if that's true."

"Oh, Mommy," said Sammy, "I'm so happy to have all these animals to play with and sleep with. I was right . . . they make me *verrry* happy."

"Good night, Sammy," said Mother, turning off the light.

"Mommy, Daddy, I can't sleep," Sammy whispered.

"What's the matter, honey?" asked Mother.

"I don't know, I just can't get comfortable," Sammy said sadly.

"Come on, Sammy," said Mother gently, "I'll take you back to your room."

Mother tucked Sammy back into bed. "Here, maybe Mr. Gorilla will help you go to sleep."

"Mommy, Daddy, I still can't sleep," Sammy cried, coming into his parents' room again. "Mr. Gorilla was no help at all. I need my old Mr. Cat, but I can't find him. There are just too many stuffed animals in my room."

"But Sammy," Mother said, "I thought you said that
if you had all these animals you'd feel happy?"

Sammy thought for a minute. "I *did* feel happy for
a while having them and playing with them all. But now
I don't care about them. I miss Mr. Cat."

"Why is Mr. Cat so important?" Mother asked softly.

"Because Mr. Cat is always with me," explained Sammy. "He took care of me when I was sick with the flu. He was with me when I was scared of the lightning and thunder. He is always there when I go to sleep and when I wake up. He really cares about me. I want Mr. Cat!"

"Here he is," said Mother. "He was pushed way under the bed. But what shall we do with all these other stuffed animals?"

"Mommy," asked Sammy sleepily, "are there some children who don't have even one Mr. Cat to love and protect them when they're scared?"

"Yes, Sammy, there are," answered Mother.

"I only need one Mr. Cat, Mommy. Let's find those children and give them each one of these toy animals so they can feel loved and protected," suggested Sammy.

"Yes, Sammy, let's do that tomorrow at the children's shelter." Mother smiled.

"So, honey, you see it's not how many *things* you have that make you happy—it's how *special* something or someone is to you that makes you happy."

"Yes, Mommy. And I have Mr. Cat, I have you, and I have Daddy. I'm very happy."